Millie-Mae

Through the
Seasons

Millie-Mae

Through the
Seasons

Natalie Marshall

Kane Miller
A DIVISION OF EDC PUBLISHING

Millie-Mae

in

Summer

The trees around Millie-Mae's house have bright green leaves. Summer has arrived.

Millie-Mae
wakes up on a bright
summer morning. It is
going to be a hot day,
so Millie-Mae chooses her
yellow dress and straw hat.

Millie-Mae is going to the beach today.
She packs her blue pail and shovel in her bag.

On her way to the beach, Millie-Mae passes a row of tall yellow sunflowers growing in the sun.

Little blue butterflies and busy yellow
bees fly among the flowers.

At the beach,
the sand is warm under
Millie-Mae's bare feet.
The water is bright blue and
there are fluffy white clouds
high up in the sky.

Millie-Mae uses her pail and shovel to build a big
sandcastle. She decorates it with shells and seaweed.

At the end
of the day, Millie-Mae
washes her face, shakes the
sand from her toes, and climbs
into bed. She gives her little bear
a big hug and goes to sleep.

Good night, Millie-Mae.
Sweet dreams.

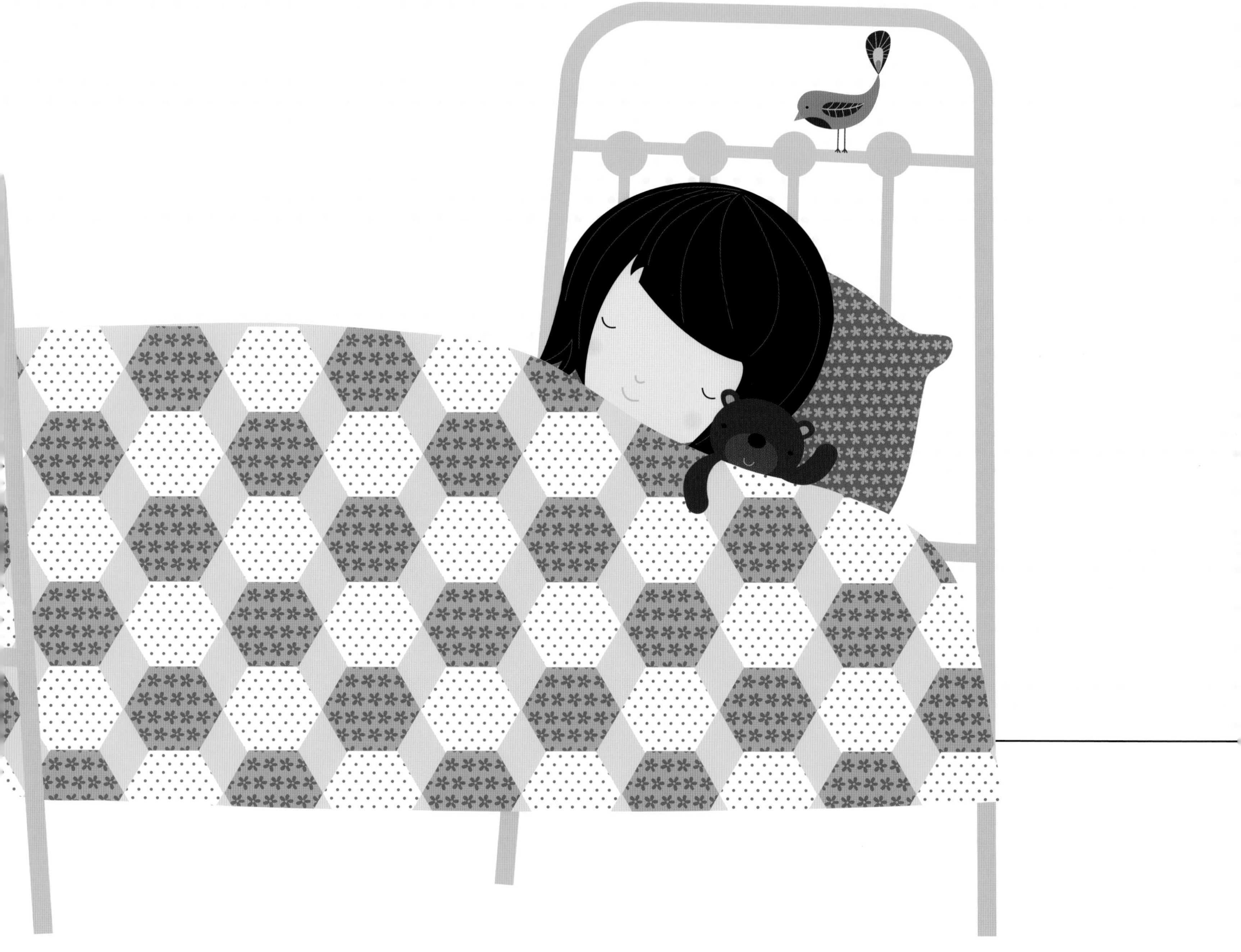

Millie-Mae
in
Autumn

Summer has become autumn. The trees around Millie-Mae's house have turned from green to red, yellow, and orange.

One cool
morning, Millie-Mae
decides to go to the park.
She wears her dress, her
warm coat, tights, and
a woollen scarf.

Millie-Mae is taking her little bear, pink rabbit, and yellow tea set in her red wagon.

The autumn wind is blowing the red, yellow,
and orange leaves high up into the air.

At the park, the
autumn leaves crunch
under Millie-Mae's shoes.
When the wind blows,
more leaves fall
from the trees.

Millie-Mae and her toys are having a tea party!

It is bedtime
for Millie-Mae.
She can hear the wind
rustling through the
autumn leaves outside
as she falls asleep.

Good night, Millie-Mae.
Sweet dreams.

Millie-Mae
in
Winter

There are no leaves left on the trees
around Millie-Mae's house. Winter has arrived.

On a snowy
winter morning,
Millie-Mae gets dressed
for the day. She chooses
her winter coat, warm
woollen hat, cozy scarf,
mittens, and boots.

Millie-Mae is very excited today.
She is going to play in the snow.

The snow is sparkling white and very cold.
It crunches beneath Millie-Mae's boots.

Millie-Mae builds three snowmen! She uses twigs
for their arms and orange carrots for their noses.

On her walk
home, it begins to
snow. The snowflakes
are cold when they
touch Millie-Mae's face.
She catches a snowflake,
but it melts away.

Millie-Mae
has had a busy day.
After dinner she has a warm
drink, gives her little bear a
big hug, and falls asleep.

Good night, Millie-Mae.
Sweet dreams.

Millie-Mae in Spring

Winter has become spring. There are pink blossoms on the trees around Millie-Mae's house.

Millie-Mae is
playing at home in the
garden today. When it
is time to get dressed, she
chooses her yellow spring dress,
pink top, and pink socks.

Out in the garden, Millie-Mae fills up her green watering can so she can water her plants.

When she
plays on her swing,
Millie-Mae feels like she
can almost touch the clouds!
As she swings, Millie-Mae can
hear baby birds cheeping in
a nest high in the tree.

It is time for
bed. The little baby
birds have gone to sleep
in their nest, and Millie-Mae
is asleep as well.

Good night, Millie-Mae.
Sweet dreams.

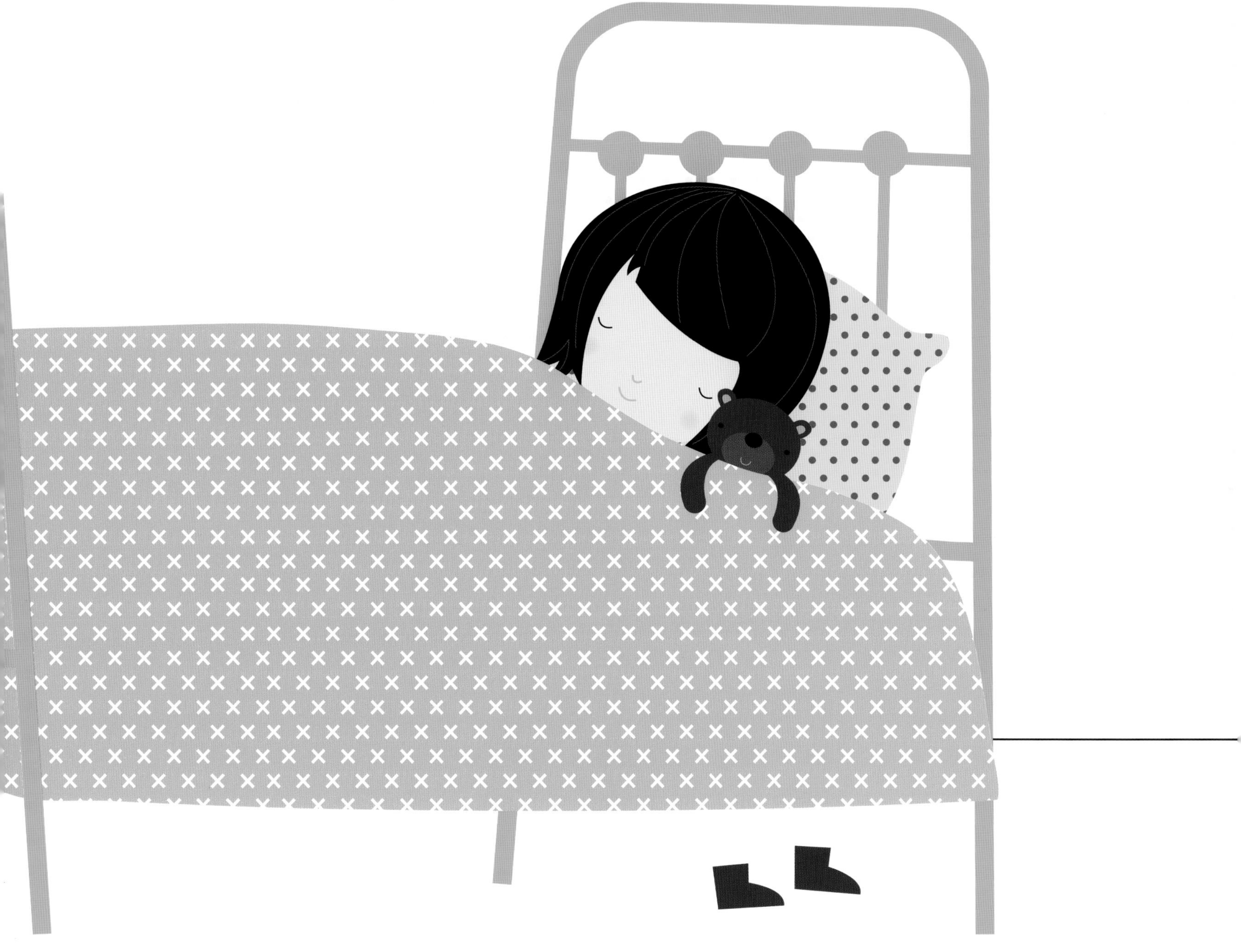

First American Edition 2021
Kane Miller, A Division of EDC Publishing

Illustration and text copyright © 2020 Natalie Marshall

First published in 2020 in Australia by Little Hare Books,
an imprint of Hardie Grant Egmont.

For information contact:
Kane Miller, A Division of EDC Publishing
P.O. Box 470663,
Tulsa, OK 74147-0663
www.kanemiller.com
www.usbornebooksandmore.com
www.edcpub.com

Library of Congress Control Number: 2020936864

Printed in Shenzhen, Guangdong Province, China
ISBN: 978-1-68464-213-7
2 3 4 5 6 7 8 9 10